UNCLE ARTHUR'S
BEDTIME STORIES

Book Five

Arthur Maxwell

*"They that be teachers shall shine
as the brightness of the firmament;
and they that turn many to righ-
teousness as the stars for ever and
ever" (Dan. 12:3, margin).*

REVIEW AND HERALD® PUBLISHING ASSOCIATION
HAGERSTOWN, MD 21740

Printed in U.S.A.

Contents

The Two Carolines 5

David's New Friend 9

The Empty Box.. 15

Mischievous Maggie 19

A Tale of Two Sparrows.................................... 23

A Brave Little Girl 29

Harry's Motor Boat 33

How the Blocks Were Put Away....................... 38

Bread From Heaven.. 41

Barbara's Talent 45

Found in the Swamp 51

How Lazy Laurie Became Mother's Helper 55

Man Overboard!.. 61

No Marks on God's Glasses 63

Shirley's Surrender 67

Why the Difference?.. 73

The Little Bird That Tells................................. 77

The Stoneboat 82

The Angel of the Books 85

Jane's Plot 89

GERTRUDE. A. STEEL.

Caroline Helping Mother After She Had Learned Her Lesson

The Two Carolines

How a Little Girl Learned That Home and Company Manners Should Be the Same

CAROLINE HERMAN was a very nice little girl in many ways. She had pretty brown hair and big brown eyes, and when she was all dressed for school in her navy-blue uniform, you would have thought, to look at her, that there wasn't a nicer little girl in all the world.

But there were two Carolines. One was the home Caroline and the other was the school Caroline. The home Caroline was left on the doorstep every morning, and picked up every dinner time when the school Caroline came back.

Now the home Caroline was a cross, pouty, grumbly, growly, and disobedient Caroline, quite unlike the Caroline that everybody saw outside and thought was such a nice little girl.

Mother was worried almost to tears over her two Carolines. What could she do? She thought it over, and devised a plan.

Now Caroline loved her school-teacher very much. Indeed, by the way she acted, it seemed she loved her teacher more than she did even her own mother. She would take her flowers and other pretty things to show her affection, and of course teacher, seeing only the school Caroline, thought she must always be a very good girl indeed.

One day the school Caroline came home and changed suddenly on the doorstep, as usual, into the home Caroline. Mother called to her as she came in,

"Will you please go round to the store and buy me some groceries?"

"No, don't want to, I'm tired," snapped the home Caroline.

However, she finally decided to go under protest.

While she was gone a visitor came to see Mrs. Herman, and being shown into the drawing room, sat down in a corner out of sight.

Caroline returned.

"Here are your old things," she said, throwing them down on the floor. "Now I'm going out to play."

"But mother's tired, wouldn't you like to help her finish her work?"

"No, I don't want to."

"Well, please lay the table for dinner."

"Don't want to."

"But you must do something to help mamma. Please lay the table, Caroline."

"I do hate laying the table," said Caroline, slamming the door, and putting on a pout that would almost frighten any one. Pulling out the tablecloth from the drawer with many grumblings, she spread it out in a rough-and-tumble sort of way. Then she brought out the knives and forks, scattered them among a few necessary dishes, and prepared to walk off.

Mother looked displeased, but did not say anything until Caroline was about to go. Then she said,

"Caroline, we are to have a visitor to dinner to-night. In fact, you might call her in now; she is in the drawing room."

Caroline's face paled. Looking round, she noticed that the drawing room door was open.

"But, mother dear,"—her tone had suddenly changed,—"the table is not set for visitors."

"No, but it is set for mother."

"But, mother, I would like to arrange it better."

"It is too late now. We must not keep our visitor waiting. Please call her in."

Very pale, and trembling a little, Caroline went into the drawing room.

"Mother says, Will you please ———"

She stopped. It was her teacher!

"O teacher, have you heard all I have been saying? Oh, dear, dear, dear!" cried Caroline, bursting into tears.

"I am sorry my little Caroline is not the same at home as she is at school," said the teacher.

"O, I'm so sorry!" wept Caroline. "I won't ever be so naughty again."

And really, to tell the truth, she never was; for always after that she could never feel quite sure that there was not some one listening to her in the next room. Mother told her, too, that

"Jesus is the unseen guest at every meal,
The silent listener to every conversation."

7

ARTHUR MAXWELL

David's New Friend

"YOU look sad, son," said mamma, as David came slouching into the kitchen with his hands in his pockets. "What's the matter?"

"Everything."

"Well, what to begin with?"

"Oh, I dunno. I suppose I'm just tired of trying to play by myself. I wish I had some friends around here, or a brother or somebody."

"You remind me of some one," said mamma, smiling at his woebegone expression.

"Who?" asked David, looking up.

"The little boy who said he felt so lonely he wanted to go into the garden and eat worms."

"Pshaw! I don't like worms," said David. "I wish we didn't live out here so far away from everybody. I want a friend who—"

"Let's go into the dining room and talk it over," said mamma, dropping the work she was doing.

David always liked to have mamma talk to him; so he welcomed the idea at once.

"Now supposing," said mamma, when she was seated, and David was leaning over the arm of her chair, "that you didn't have a friend in the world—no daddy, no mamma, just nobody at all—and then some one came along and told you that you could choose any friend you pleased out of all the people in the world—what sort of friend would you choose?"

David thought a moment, with a puzzled look on his face.

9

"Some one who would play with me," he said finally.

"But you would hardly put that first," said mamma. "Wouldn't you choose some one who would be good and kind and truthful?"

"I suppose I would," said David.

"And wouldn't you want a faithful friend, some one who would not only be your friend today, but remain your friend all through life?"

"Um," grunted David. " 'Spect so."

"And I suppose you would choose some one trustworthy, who would never tell your secrets to anybody, and never let you down in any way?"

"Yes."

"And you would want him to be strong, so that he could help you and maybe protect you from harm someday?"

"I think I'd like that, too," said David.

"And what else would you like your friend to be?"

"Rich," said David.

Mamma smiled. "That would be nice, of course, provided he was generous and unselfish," she said. "Anything else?"

"Can't think of anything else," said David.

"But you would like to have a friend like this—good, kind, truthful, faithful, trustworthy, strong, and maybe rich, too?"

"Surely," said David. "But there's nobody around like that."

"But there is," said mamma.

"Where? Who is it?" asked David.

"Let me tell you," said mamma. "The Bible tells us of a Friend who 'sticketh closer than a brother'—Some One who loves us all so much that He is willing to be everybody's friend, your friend and my friend, too, David. And you know who it is, don't you?"

David's face had taken on that faraway look again, and he said nothing.

"Well, He is just everything a friend should be," mamma went on. "And the more we know Him, the better we love Him. Do you know His name?"

"I suppose you mean Jesus," said David.

"That's right, dear," said mamma. "And let's think for a moment what a wonderful friend He is. First of all He is a very *kind* friend. He must be, for when long ago He looked down from His glorious throne in heaven and saw all the sadness and the sickness and the quarreling in this poor old world, He said, 'I must go down and help those poor people and show them a better way.' So He left His throne and came down to this earth as a little baby and grew up as any boy does, so that He would know just everything about little boys and the things that little boys like best, and how lonely they get sometimes.

"Then He went about making all the sick people better, helping the blind to see and the deaf to hear, and saying all the nicest things He could to everybody all the time. You see, He wanted them to know how much He loved them and how He wanted to be their friend.

"Then some cruel people took a dislike to Him and didn't want Him for a friend, and finally killed Him. But even when they were treating Him so cruelly, He prayed for them and said He forgave them.

"After that He rose from the dead and went back to heaven to sit upon His throne of glory once more; but He did not forget the people He had left behind here. Through all the years He has loved them, and loves us all today, and wants to be your friend, too. And that proves that He is not only a kind friend, but a *faithful* friend. His love has never faded the tiniest bit. And in some wonderful way He knows all about every little boy and girl that is born, and watches over them, if they want Him to, all their lives.

"Then Jesus is a very *wise* friend, too; and it's good to have a wise friend, you know, David—some one who knows everything and can answer all your questions."

"Does Jesus really know everything?" asked David.

"Surely He does," said mamma.

"How?" asked David.

"Well," said mamma, "even since He went back to heaven He has lived nearly two thousand years. And before He came here, He lived 'from everlasting,' and nobody, I suppose, will ever know just how long that is. If you think back millions and millions of years, you will never get to the beginning of it. So, David, any one who has lived as long as that must be very, very wise, don't you think? And that reminds me of something else about Jesus. He is a very *strong* friend.

"You said just now that you wanted a strong friend, and there's nobody so strong as Jesus. The Bible tells us that He made all this great wide, wonderful world— all the mountains and the seas, the flowers and the trees, the animals and the fishes, and all the people, too. He created the first parents of every living thing on the earth today. He also made the sun, the moon, and the millions and millions of stars."

"How could He do all that?" asked David.

"He just spoke, and it happened," said mamma. "That's what the Bible says. And mustn't it have been marvelous to see star after star blaze out in the sky as He called each one into existence!"

"Like fireworks," whispered David.

"Yes," said mamma. "The most glorious fireworks ever seen. And this only goes to prove how strong a friend He is. Seeing that He made everything, and keeps the whole universe running smoothly as a clock, He must be very strong indeed. That is why He says to us, 'Is there anything too hard for the Lord?' "

"He must be a *rich* friend, too," said David.

"He is," said mamma. "Ever so rich. In fact, there is no end to His riches. All the gold and silver in the world really belong to Him, with all the diamonds, the rubies, and every other precious stone, for He made them all. And we don't know how much more He has stored away in the stars. With such a wealthy friend, we should never worry about what we need."

"What other sort of friend is He?" asked David.

"Well, I should say He is a very patient and long-suffering friend," said mamma. "We all do many things that displease Him, but just as soon as we tell Him we're sorry, why, He forgives us and is just as friendly as ever afterward. And that's so different from the way many earthly friends treat us. Oftentimes, just as soon as we annoy them, they get upset and run away and never speak to us any more. But Jesus doesn't treat us that way. He is 'the same yesterday, and today, and forever,' and it's a great comfort to have a friend who never changes in His love.

"Then, one of the best things of all about Jesus is the fact that He is an ever-present Friend. You used to have little friends living next door, but they have gone away, and you may not see them again for years. But Jesus doesn't go away like that. He is always with us."

"How can He be?" asked David.

"By His Holy Spirit," said mamma. "All we have to do is to tell Him that we love Him and want Him to be our friend. Then He will come into our minds and hearts by His Holy Spirit, and we shall feel His presence with us all the time. We will think about Him and talk to Him, and sometimes, maybe, hear Him talking to us. And so we shall never be lonely."

"Never be lonely," repeated David, slowly.

"No, never," said mamma. "Just thinking about Jesus and His love, and trying to please Him by doing His work and helping the people He wants to help—this will keep us always happy."

"Is that why you always look so happy?" asked David.

"Why, yes, of course it is," said mamma. "And Jesus is whispering to you, David, just now, 'Let's be friends.'"

And mamma smiled such a beautiful smile and spoke so softly and lovingly that the frown suddenly disappeared from David's brow, and the peace and joy that were in mamma's heart overflowed into his.

Jesus had found a new friend.

And so had David.

The Empty Box

OH, the excitement!

Basil and Vera had been invited to stay at their uncle's farm, and mother had said yes!

They were going to be gone for a month.

A whole month!

Immediately the house was in an uproar as preparations began for the great and glorious holiday. What planning, what packing, what happy dreaming!

At last the day of departure arrived. Uncle had come for them himself, and soon his car looked like a freight car, piled up with bags and suitcases as it was.

Then came the good-bys.

Basil and Vera hadn't thought about that before. It was wonderful to go away, but just terrible to leave mother, and all alone, too.

Basil swallowed hard, and Vera wiped some tears away.

"Don't forget to write to me," said mother, doing a little "weep" herself as she tried hard to appear happy.

"Oh, sure," cried Basil, "we won't forget."

"We'll write every day," said Vera.

And off they went.

Two days later a postcard arrived to say that they had had a nice trip and had reached the farm safely.

That was all.

Morning by morning and evening by evening mother would go down to the mailbox near the front gate, hoping and hoping that there might be a letter—or even a little

postcard—from the children; but there was none. Soon she began to worry lest some accident might have happened to them, or, worse still, lest they had just forgotten.

Which they had.

Life on the farm proved to be so full of interest from early morning till late at night that Basil and Vera felt they just didn't have time to write home. There were so many other children there about their own age, so many places to visit, so many games to play, that they never thought another thing about mother.

"She won't mind," said Basil one day when Vera said she thought it was about time they wrote. "She knows we're all right; so why bother? Anyway, there isn't time now. We have to get ready for the party."

When a letter arrived from mother, they would say, "We'll have to write tomorrow." But "tomorrow" never came. It was always like that. No time. Too busy.

So the month slipped by.

Meanwhile, twice a day, mother walked down to the box and back again with her heart as heavy as lead. The box was always empty. "So," she would say to herself, "they have forgotten so soon! They don't care enough to write." She worried herself ill over it, and the doctor had to come. Somehow he guessed what was the trouble, and, knowing the children well, dropped them a line himself.

Basil and Vera were horrified.

Mother ill! Why, that was terrible. Worried because they had not written her!

They decided to write at once. And what a letter it was! They made it up together, and told mother how much they loved her, how they wished she was with them, and how they were longing to see her again.

Then one day mother, slowly opening the mailbox, saw a white envelope inside. A letter from the children!

It acted like a powerful medicine.

She felt better immediately, and phoned the doctor he need not come again.

If only Basil and Vera had written before! What a lot of sadness they might have saved! What a lot of happiness they might have given!

For there is no disappointment quite so keen and heartbreaking as that of finding a constantly empty mailbox.

Is somebody somewhere looking in an empty box for a letter from you?

Did I hear you say yes?

Then sit down and write that letter now.

ARTHUR MAXWELL

Mischievous Maggie

And How She Learned to Be Good

LITTLE Maggie McClements was perhaps the most mischievous child who ever lived. She used to do the most dreadful things that any little girl could ever think of. Such good little children as you could not imagine the pranks she would play, and I hardly dare tell you for fear you will do the same. Why, once when she had lost her skipping rope, she went into the back garden when mamma was out shopping, and climbing on one of the dining room chairs, cut off a piece of the clothesline! What happened when mamma returned home, I'm sure you wouldn't want me to say.

Then one day — I must tell you about this — daddy discovered little Miss Maggie sitting on the kitchen table cleaning his shoes with *stove polish!* Poor daddy didn't know whether to laugh or to be cross. However, as he loved his little girl very much, he said to himself that probably Maggie thought she was trying to help him. But it was a long time before the shoes looked right again.

Another day she tried to find where the noise came from in the alarm clock. She managed to get the clock to pieces, but no one could ever put it together again! Did you ever hear of such a little girl in all your life?

There seemed no end to Maggie's mischief. It just bubbled out of her. Mamma and daddy would often say to each other that they wondered

what would happen to her when she grew up. What to do for her they did not know. But it turned out that Maggie cured herself.

Daddy had bought a fine new camera, of which he was very proud. But to no one, not even to daddy, was it of more interest than to little Miss Maggie herself.

Right away, in fact almost before the camera was unpacked, she wanted daddy to take her photograph. He said he could not possibly do so till the sun was up the next morning. So Maggie was up with the sun to have her picture taken. She was very anxious indeed to have a really good picture, as she wanted to show it to the little girl next door, whose daddy had often taken *her* photograph. There was a keen sense of rivalry in Maggie, and she did hope that her picture would look prettier than that of the next-door girl.

Well, daddy took the photograph — in fact he took six of them, showing Maggie in all sorts of positions. Maggie was delighted, and looked forward to getting the prints.

Daddy went off to his work and left the camera on his writing table, telling Maggie that he would get the pictures developed when he returned.

But Maggie, mischievous as ever, could not wait so long for her pictures. She did not see why she could not take them out of the camera just as well as daddy; and he surely would be pleased to see them when he got back.

So little Miss Maggie sat down at the table and began to look at the camera. How to open it she did not know, but she pulled and pushed at it until at last her finger accidentally touched a little button on the side and the back fell out. Maggie was delighted, and felt sure she would now quickly find her pictures. Inside was a long strip of black paper and underneath it another strip of queer-looking white paper that looked something like the stuff of which her celluloid doll was made. She pulled all this out, but still there seemed to be no pictures. The box was empty.

Maggie was very much disappointed, and felt sure daddy must have made a mistake. Then she tried to put the paper back inside so that daddy should find it as he left it; but somehow it wouldn't go, and the more she worked at it, the worse it became, until finally she gave up in despair.

Maybe you can guess what happened when daddy got back from work.

Anyhow, after Maggie had stopped crying, daddy explained to her how she had spoiled all his pictures, and that she could never see the ones he had taken that morning — that they were all on that queer-looking strip of white " paper," waiting to be developed, but because of her naughtiness, they would never be seen by any one.

Maggie was so disappointed she said that she would never do it again, and that after this she really would try to be good. And while she did not always keep her promise, it is a fact that the lesson she learned that day remained with her ever after.

A Tale of Two Sparrows

MR. and Mrs. Sparrow were just married, and they were looking for a nice place where they could build their nest.

They flew about for a long time without any success. Mrs. Sparrow was rather hard to please. Whenever Mr. Sparrow found a nice little corner that he thought would do splendidly, and came swooping down through the air to tell her so, Mrs. Sparrow would say, "Oh, that's not at all suitable for me, Mr. Sparrow. I must have something much better than that for my home."

At last Mr. Sparrow got so discouraged that he said he wouldn't look any more, and that Mrs. Sparrow, if she were so particular, had better look for herself.

Mrs. Sparrow took him at his word, and said that if she couldn't find a nice place in half the time that Mr. Sparrow had taken, she would know the reason why.

So off flew Mrs. Sparrow to see what she could do.

In a little while she returned.

"I've found a wonderful place," she said. "It's warm and cozy, well protected from the weather, and the way in is so small that no one else will ever be able to find it; so we shall be quite by ourselves, with no neighbors to annoy us. You'll be able to sleep late in the morning, for there will be no others birds around to start singing too early."

"My dear!" cried Mr. Sparrow, "where can it be? Do show me at once. I'm so glad you have been so successful."

"Ah," said Mrs. Sparrow, "it takes me to find a home. I'll show you. You come along with me."

With that Mrs. Sparrow hopped off her perch and flew high in the air, with Mr. Sparrow following meekly at a respectful distance behind.

On and on they flew.

"Where are you taking me?" asked Mr. Sparrow, getting alarmed.

"You'll find out in a minute," said Mrs. Sparrow.

They were approaching a lofty church tower, and Mrs. Sparrow seemed to be flying to the very top of it.

"My dear, do be careful," called Mr. Sparrow. "This is very dangerous."

Mrs. Sparrow flew on as if she did not hear him. At last she alighted where a small window had been broken at the top of the tower. In a moment she had popped inside.

Poor Mr. Sparrow followed, very much alarmed and wondering what terrible thing would happen to them.

"Look," said Mrs. Sparrow. "Isn't this ideal? The very thing we have been looking for! Dry, fairly clean, and very private. I told you, Mr. Sparrow, that I would find the right place."

"But, my dear," said poor Mr. Sparrow, greatly agitated, "do you think it's all right? Is it quite safe?"

"Safe!" cried Mrs. Sparrow. "Of course it's safe. Now please get busy and bring all the straw you can find. We might as well make ourselves comfortable as soon as we can."

Very meekly Mr. Sparrow obeyed. In a little while he was back again, bringing a few pieces of straw in his beak. By this time Mrs. Sparrow had selected an attractive spot for the nest in between a number of wooden pipes. Mr. Sparrow put down his pieces of straw and went out in search of more.

It did not take them very long to build their nest, and in a day or two they were quite settled down, ready to enjoy a well-earned rest.

All at once something terrible happened. It was on a Wednesday evening about seven o'clock. Mr. and Mrs. Sparrow were settled nice and comfortable in bed when suddenly they were awakened by a terrific noise. Groans and roars came from the big pipes, whines and shrieks from the little pipes. The whole place rocked and shook.

"My dear! My dear!" cried Mr. Sparrow. "What's the matter? What can have happened? Are you quite safe?"

But Mrs. Sparrow was not there to hear. Already she was at the broken window, shrieking at Mr. Sparrow to escape for his life. And without another thought they both jumped from the top of the tower out into the dark, cold night.

Probably those poor little sparrows will never know what really happened that terrible evening. As long as they live they will tell their friends how they lost their beautiful home, recounting in awed whispers the terrors they suffered in the haunted tower.

The fact was, of course, that they had merely tried to make their nest in the church organ loft. And the awful sounds they had heard that Wednesday evening were really the hymns the organist was playing for the prayer meeting.

To the people in the church the music was beautiful. "How lovely!" they all had said. "What delightful harmonies! What a wonderful organist!"

But to the poor little sparrows in the loft it had seemed like an earthquake and a hurricane combined.

All of which goes to tell us that things are not always what they seem. And sometimes children, like the sparrows, are frightened merely because they do not understand. And sometimes, too, they grumble and growl because they are not yet old enough to appreciate the meaning of things beyond them.

Perhaps you have heard a little boy say sometime, "I don't like going to church. I never can understand a word the preacher says, and some of the hymns have no tune to them at all." Some day, however, he will understand the preacher and rejoice in his inspiring words. And some day the hymns that have seemed to have the least "tune" in them will be loved and prized most of all.

Perhaps, too, you have heard a little girl say, "I don't know why I have to put up with so much. I don't have the nice things other children have, and I'm always getting sick."

That *is* hard to understand, I admit. But when you feel like that, just think that Some One is playing on the organ of your life. To you the notes sound harsh and discordant; but the Organist knows what He is playing, and some day you will understand how lovely was the tune that He composed.

So when things go wrong and you are tempted to judge quickly and unkindly, just wait a little while and think of the sparrows in the tower.

Illus. Lond. News   L. P. Robert, Artist

Sparrows at Home

A Brave Little Girl

TALKING about birds reminds me of another true bird story with a really thrilling adventure.

Dick, a very pretty canary, belonged to a little girl called Minnie, who lived in the country with her father and mother.

Dick had been a birthday present to Minnie and she loved him very much indeed. Although she had a beautiful golden cage for him, yet Dick was often allowed out and would perch on Minnie's shoulder, or on the side of her plate at mealtimes. Minnie had only to whistle quietly to start Dick off in a riot of glorious song that filled the whole house with music.

Then one day Dick disappeared. His cage door was open, and no Dick was to be seen. Minnie searched the house from top to bottom, but all in vain. Then she went out into the garden and peered into all the bushes, listening for any little "Cheep, cheep!" that might reveal the presence of her precious birdie. But still no Dick was to be found.

Minnie talked very seriously to the dog and the cat. Indeed she had grave suspicions about them, especially pussy, but both professed absolute innocence.

Three days passed, and still no Dick appeared. Poor little Minnie was heart-broken, for she felt that never again would she be able to get a bird so tame and loving as her dear little Dick.

Then one morning a neighbour called. "I think I know where your canary is," she said.

"Do you really?" cried Minnie. "Where, where?"

"Come with me and I will show you," said the neighbour. "I think I heard him calling."

"Let's go at once," said Minnie, dashing out of the house and dragging the neighbour with her.

"This way," said the lady, walking in the direction of the well. They reached the edge and looked over, Minnie holding tightly to the neighbour's hand. "Listen!"

They both listened. Then from far down in the darkness they heard a faint "Cheep! cheep!"

"It's Dick, it's Dick!" cried Minnie. "My poor little Dick! However shall we get him out?"

"Let's go and tell Father," said the neighbour. "Perhaps he will think of a way."

They both ran back to the house.

"We've found him!" cried Minnie. "He is down at the bottom of the well. How shall we get him out?"

"I'm afraid it's impossible," said Father. "It's very deep, and I haven't a ladder nearly long enough to reach to the bottom."

"But we can't leave Dick there," cried Minnie. "Let me go down and fetch him."

"You go down the well!" cried Father.

"Yes, I'll go. You let me down in the bucket, then I'll pick him up and you can pull me to the top again."

"We couldn't do that," said Father.

"But we must," said Minnie. "It will be quite all right. Do, Daddy, come on! Let's go now before Dick dies."

Minnie was so in earnest that Father relented and

the three walked over to the well together. Again they looked down the deep, dark hole.

"Are you sure you want to go down there?" said Father.

"Yes, yes, of course," said brave little Minnie. "Can't you hear Dick calling me?"

Then without another word she stepped into the bucket. Father tied the rope very tightly around her, so that there was no possibility of her slipping out. Then, very, very carefully, he lowered her over the edge.

Down, down, down, went Minnie. Oh, how dark it was! But as she descended so Dick's little "Cheep! cheep!" became louder and louder. It seemed as though he guessed Minnie was coming to his rescue. And Minnie didn't mind the dark a bit for she was so anxious to save her little friend.

Splash! At last the bucket touched the water and Father stopped paying out the rope.

"Dick! Dick!" cried Minnie, peering through the darkness. Yes, there was the poor, frightened little bird, perched on a little ledge on the side of the well. She reached out her hands with joy and picked him up, signalling to her father to pull them both to the top again.

Up, up, up, they went together, and at last they were out in the sunshine once again and Father was clasping his brave little girl in his arms.

"But weren't you afraid?" he said to her.

"Of course I wasn't!" she replied. "I knew you were holding the rope."

"Well," said Father, as he was telling the story at home that evening, "I hope we shall always trust our heavenly Father as Minnie trusted me."

Harry's Motor Boat

THE great dream of his life had come true. For years and years, so it seemed, Harry had longed for a real motor boat, one that would go all by itself without having to be wound up; and now at last it had come. Only this very morning his uncle had brought one for him as a birthday present. What joy and rejoicing of heart!

First of all, of course, it had to be tried in the bath, just to see if it really would " go." But after Harry had seen it get up steam and go up and down the bath a score of times, he could not rest until he had taken it to the lake.

So, armed with a bottle of methylated spirits, a box of matches, and his precious boat, he started off.

" You *will* be careful, won't you? " said mother.

" Of course," said Harry.

" And be sure to be back by six o'clock? "

" Yes, mother."

And away he went.

What fun he did have! What a joy it was to watch the little engine getting up steam until at last, amid much fizzing and spluttering, the piston gave its first jerk and the propeller began to spin merrily round!

Away went the little boat across the lake, while Harry rushed round in his bare feet to meet it at the other side. So excited was he that he walked into the water to meet it coming in. Turning it round, he sent it off again, this time toward a different spot. He was surprised how far the boat would go with one " filling-up," and every time it came to land he tried to make it go still farther.

Time goes quickly when one is happy, and Harry did not notice how the hours were slipping by. At last, however, lengthening shadows aroused him, and he stopped a passer-by to ask him the time.

" Half-past five."

" Phew ! " whistled Harry. " I'll have to be packing up soon. Just time for one more trip."

But how often it happens that the " one more " that is really " one too many " ends in tragedy!

Anyway, so it happened with poor Harry. For the last trip he decided to send the boat the longest possible journey. If it reached the point aimed at, he thought, it would be quite near to the footpath that led toward home. So, he argued, it would really save time if he made the last trip the longest.

Steam up once more, away she went merrily on her " transatlantic " crossing, with Harry's delighted eyes following her every inch of the way.

" She's half way across! " he muttered to himself.

Then his heart seemed to stand still. The motor boat had stopped. He felt sure it had stopped. There was no sign of movement, although he thought he could see steam coming out of the safety-valve. Yes, it had really stopped.

What had happened, he could not tell. Perhaps he had used the boat too much for one afternoon; perhaps it needed oil, perhaps, dreadful thought, it had caught in some weeds. Poor Harry did not know. He stood there on the bank with eyes glued on the boat, hoping against hope that it would start again. But it did not move. That it had caught on something he became convinced. How could he get it back?   Far in the distance he heard a factory whistle.

"That's the five-to-six whistle," he said to himself, "and I must be home at six!"

Poor Harry! What should he do? He *must* keep his promise to his mother, for he always did, but if he went away, some one would be sure to get the boat before he could return. In desperation he walked into the water as far as he dared go, but he found that it suddenly became very deep just a few yards from the shore, and he had to return.

Again he looked at the little boat, quietly bobbing up and down in the middle of the lake.   Then he thought of the time.

"Oh, what shall I do?" he thought.

There was no one about to whom he could appeal for help, for the few who had been there in the afternoon had already gone home.   Of a sudden an unusual thought came into his mind.   Some of you may smile when I tell you what it was.   It was the music of a hymn he had sung in church a few days before.   Presently the words came back to him.

> "What a Friend we have in Jesus,
>   All our sins and griefs to bear!
> What a privilege to carry
>   Everything to God in prayer."

"But," Harry said to himself, "surely Jesus isn't interested in my little motor boat!" He almost smiled at the thought.   Then in his desperate anxiety he said, "Why not?   Perhaps He is."   And right there by the lake side Harry shut his eyes just for a second, and asked Jesus to look after his little boat while he ran home to keep his promise to his mother.

Taking one last, loving look at his precious boat, he turned away and ran home as fast as he could go.

He was a few minutes late, but mother said nothing about it, for she saw at once that he was greatly distressed. When she learned that he had even left his boat behind in the lake in order to keep his promise to her, she felt very proud of him indeed.

" After supper," she said, " we will both go back, even though it is dark, and see what we can do with a ball of string."

Supper did not take long, I can assure you, and by half past seven Harry and his mother were on their way back to the lake, with a lantern, and string enough to stretch across.

By the time they arrived, a pale moon was rising, casting its rays across the silent waters.

Eagerly they both strained their eyes to see the little boat.

" It was over there," said Harry, " right in the middle."

" I can't see it," said mother.

" Neither can I," said Harry, with a trace of fear in his voice.

" Perhaps when the moon gets up a bit ——" began mother with a note of encouragement.

" No," said Harry disconsolately, " it's gone. I know just where it was. It must have sunk."

They walked all around the lake, hoping perchance it might have drifted ashore, but to no purpose. Nowhere was there any trace of it.

" No good! " sighed Harry. " Let's go home."

And in his heart he said, " And what was the good of asking Jesus to look after it? "

" Crunch! "

Heavy footsteps on the gravel behind startled them both.

" Hello! " said a deep voice, " and what are you doing here in the dark? "

It was the gamekeeper.

" I lost my motor boat this afternoon," said Harry, " and mother and I have come down to look for it."

" Have you found it? " said the man, more kindly.

" No, we haven't," said Harry.

" Shouldn't think you had," he said, " in the dark. It's late now. You'd better follow me."

Something strange in his tone of voice caused Harry's hopes to rise again.

They turned and followed the old man along the lake shore once more. Presently they reached an old boathouse. The gamekeeper stopped, pulled out a bunch of keys, and opened the door.

" Bring the lantern over here," he said.

Mother held it forward, and its rays fell full on — the precious motor boat!

" There it is, there it is! " cried Harry. " How did you get it? "

" Never mind about that," said the old man. " I've got an old boat here and two eyes in my head."

" Thank you ever so much! " said Harry, as he and mother said good night to the gamekeeper. Then they hurried homeward, Harry gripping the motor boat as though there were danger of his losing it again.

And on the way his heart sent up a silent thanksgiving to the Friend who never forgets a request and who even answers the prayer of a boy for his boat.

How the Blocks Were Put Away

"BEDTIME!" called mamma. "Put the blocks away, dears."

"No! No! No!" cried the children in a chorus of disapproval.

"Don't want to go to bed," said Jimmie, the youngest.

"It's so early," said Gerald; "I'm not tired."

"And I'm not going to put the blocks away," said Sheila, "because I didn't put them out."

"And I didn't," said Gerald.

"And I didn't," repeated Jimmie.

"But you can't leave the dining room looking like this," said mamma. "Daddy will be coming home soon, and he always likes to see the place tidy."

"Well, I'm not going to put the things away," said Gerald. "That's Sheila's job."

"It's not my job, mamma. I think Gerald's mean; he should do it himself."

"I can't do it," said Jimmie with a sigh, "for I'm too tired."

"Well," said mamma, "somebody must do it; and I will give you just five minutes to decide. If the blocks are not away then — well, you know what will happen."

So mamma went into the kitchen and closed the door behind her. The three children sat on the floor and looked at the pile of blocks. Then they scowled at one another.

" You should put them away," said Sheila to Gerald. " You're mean."

" So are you. I shan't do it, so there," and Gerald pulled his feet up under him and locked his hands over his knees in an attitude of grim obstinacy.

Slowly the minutes ticked away.

" Mamma will be here in two minutes, and then you'll catch it," said Sheila.

" So will you."

" But it's your job," insisted Sheila.

" It isn't; it's yours," replied Gerald.

Sheila looked at the clock.

" There's only another minute," she said; " and you know mamma always does what she says."

" Well, put the things away, then."

" I won't; it's your job."

" It isn't; it's yours."

" I'll tell you what," interrupted little Jimmie. " Let's each put one away, one after the other; and I'll start."

" Not a bad idea, Jimmie," said Gerald.

So Jimmie brought the box and put in the first block. Sheila followed with another, and then Gerald. Soon they were trying to see who could pick up the blocks quickest. Before the last minute had gone, all the blocks were put away.

When mamma came in, they were all smiling and happy; and when they saw the slipper that mamma held in her right hand, they were very glad they had taken Jimmie's suggestion.

Bread From Heaven

"WELL, it's pretty hard," said father, "and I don't see the way through; but I still feel sure that God will help us."

"I hope He will—soon," said mother earnestly, knowing how very little food there was left in the pantry.

"I never was in such a fix before," father went on. "No money in the house at all, and through no fault of our own, either. I wonder what is going to happen."

"I can't tell," said mother. "It's the children I'm worried about. They'll all be in for supper in a minute or two, and there isn't a bite of bread for them."

"Is the last loaf gone?" asked father anxiously.

"It is," replied mother sadly, "the last loaf."

"Then it is surely time for God to work," said father.

At this moment the back door was flung open with a bang, and in rushed the three children, panting from their run up the long hill from school, and, as usual, desperately hungry.

"What's for supper, mamma?" asked the eldest.

Mother looked at father. For a moment she didn't know just what to say.

"I'm afraid," she said, "God hasn't sent it yet."

The children's faces fell. Nothing to eat! Phew! That was awful.

They knew father was out of work, and that he was having a very hard time, but there had always been something for them; they had never before had to go without.

"Mamma," said the youngest, after a pause, "if there isn't any food in the house, why don't we ask Jesus to send us some? I'm sure He won't let us starve, and I'm so hungry."

"It's the only thing we can do," said father. "Let's gather round the table now and pray."

So without another word they all knelt down, father, mother, and the three children, and pleaded with God to send them at least some bread to eat as He had promised.

Now it so happened that this very afternoon two ladies, who belonged to the same church as this family, were talking about them, wondering why they had not seen them of late.

"I think there must be something the matter," said one, "or they would surely have been to the meeting yesterday."

"You're right," said the other. "I think we should go to visit them, and find out if there is anything they need. The husband has been out of work for some time, I believe."

"Yes," said the first lady. "Let us go now."

A few minutes later the two ladies set out for the little cottage in the country where the poor family lived.

It was quite a distance to walk, part of the way being up a long, steep hill.

They had nearly reached the top of the hill when a baker's truck passed them, traveling very swiftly. As it went by, what do you suppose happened? Well, believe it or not, the door of the truck flew open, and out fell a loaf of bread on the roadway. A moment later the truck seemed to hit a stone or a rut in the road, for it shook violently, scattering loaves in all directions through the open door.

Quite unaware of what had happened, the driver of the truck continued his headlong course, and in a few seconds was out of sight and far away.

Here was a problem for the two ladies. All over the road were beautiful, brown, crusty loaves of bread, good food that in a few minutes would be crushed and spoiled by other traffic passing by. It seemed too bad to leave them there, and as the truck driver did not return, they decided to pick them up.

It took them a little while to do it, but at last they stood there on the grass beside the road, each with a pile of loaves in her arms.

"What shall we do with them now?" asked one of the ladies, smiling, but a little worried.

"I don't know," laughed the other. "If we knew who owned them, we'd take them back to him; but we don't. The only thing I can think of is to take them with us and see what comes of it."

"Well, let's do it, then," said the other, "and quickly, for my arms are getting tired."

So off they went, soon reaching the garden gate of the little cottage they had set out to find. Walking up the path, the loaves still piled high in their arms, they knocked at the door.

Rat-tat-tat!

The door was opened by mother, and the two

ladies saw a sight that moved their hearts, for there were father and the three children still kneeling in prayer around the empty table.

A moment later all were on their feet, their eyes gleaming with surprise and excitement.

"Jesus has sent us bread!" cried the youngest. "I knew He would, if we asked Him."

"Yes," said father, "He surely has, and far more than we dared to ask for. It is bread from heaven indeed."

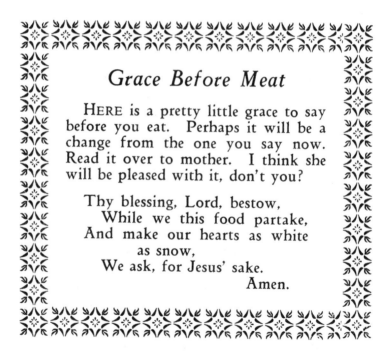

Grace Before Meat

HERE is a pretty little grace to say before you eat. Perhaps it will be a change from the one you say now. Read it over to mother. I think she will be pleased with it, don't you?

Thy blessing, Lord, bestow,
    While we this food partake,
And make our hearts as white
    as snow,
    We ask, for Jesus' sake.
                            Amen.

Barbara's Talent

"MOTHER!" gasped Barbara, rushing into the dining room and flopping down in an armchair, "I've got to earn some money."

"My dear!" exclaimed mother. "Whatever is the matter with the child now!"

"Yes, I must," went on Barbara. "It's most important, and I have got to earn a lot very quickly."

Mother began to look serious.

"What for?" she asked.

"Well," said Barbara very excitedly, "Mr. Walters, the new superintendent, told us in Sabbath school this morning that if we didn't give $250 for missions within the next two weeks, Mr. James would have to come back from India right away."

"Why, we've only just sent him out," said mother.

"I know; that's just the trouble," said Barbara. "Mr. Walters said that everybody thought there would be enough money to keep him there. But there isn't. Something's gone wrong, he said, and the Mission Board is very hard up. So there, if we don't raise the $250 in two weeks—well, Mr. James comes home."

"That sounds very serious," said mother. "But, Barbara dear, we can't raise $250 in just two weeks."

"Oh, no," said Barbara, "not we by ourselves. Each class has agreed to raise $25. Each one in the class has promised to raise $2.50."

"Have you promised $2.50?" gasped mother.

"Why, of course," said Barbara. "I couldn't do anything else, could I? And that's why I've got to earn some money. How can I do it, mother dear?"

"Well," said mother, "it's all very well for you to promise money like that, but I haven't got it to give you, dear, even if you help me ever such a lot. You know daddy has not been earning very much lately."

"I know," said Barbara, on the verge of tears, "but I—surely—can—earn it—somehow. Er—er I must keep my—er—promise, now I've made it."

Barbara began to cry.

"Never mind, dear," said mother, "we'll find some way out, surely. But you have taken on a difficult task, and no mistake."

"I did so want to help," said Barbara.

"I'm sure you did," said mother, putting her arm round Barbara's neck. "Let's think it over awhile and see what can be done."

That evening, as the family gathered round the fire for prayers, mother read to them the parable of the talents. As the story proceeded, Barbara's face grew more and more serious. She could see the man with the five talents trading with them and earning five talents more to give to the King. Then she saw the man with the two talents earning two talents. And then she saw the man with one talent burying it in the earth and having nothing —nothing—to give to the Lord at His return.

She became very serious.

"What's troubling you, dear?" asked mother, as she closed the Book.

"Oh, I feel just like the man with one talent who didn't earn anything at all. Only there's just this difference, that I don't have *one* talent."

"Well, Barbara, I didn't think you would take it so much to heart. And you have talents, many of them."

"No, I haven't. I haven't any at all. I'm just no good, and I'll never be able to earn that money."

"O Barbara, don't be so despondent. You certainly have one talent anyway, and perhaps God will help you to use that to His glory."

"I'm sure I haven't," said Barbara.

"You have forgotten your voice," said mother. "You know how beautifully you can sing when you want to. Perhaps—who knows?—you may be able to keep your promise by singing for Jesus."

"Me?" said Barbara. "How could I? No one would listen to a little girl like me."

"I'm not so sure," said mother. "You seem to have forgotten that it is nearly Christmas time, and people will listen to children then, you know —that is, if they sing nicely and reverently."

"Do you mean that I could go out and sing carols at people's houses?"

"Well, not by yourself exactly. But I've got an idea. Here's Richard with his violin, and Bessie —she can sing too. I believe that the three of you might do wonderfully well. At any rate we could think about it."

A new light entered Barbara's eyes. Hope stirred anew within her little heart. That $2.50 she had promised seemed nearer than it had since she reached home.

All next day they talked over mother's idea, and in the evening the three children had a practice together, with mother at the piano. They soon found that they could get along very well with several simple hymns, and this made them full of eagerness to see what they could do outside.

Two evenings later they started out. And what a happy time they did have! Barbara sang as she had never sung at home. She felt she was using her one talent for Jesus. People opened their windows to listen to the clear, musical little voice that rang out on the still evening air. Richard's violin was a wonderful help, and Bessie helped a lot as well. She knocked at the doors and told the story of how they were all trying to gather money so that their missionary would not have to be brought back from India. No one could resist her sweet little smile. At every house she received something. One lady gave five cents, another ten cents, and one happy old gentleman brought a quarter out of his trousers pocket.

When at last they all reached home, they were so excited and happy that mother scarcely knew what to do with them. After counting up their money, they found they had collected ninety-four cents.

"Why!" exclaimed Barbara, "we shall have to go out only three or four times to get more than I promised."

"It's wonderful," said mother. "I prayed that God would bless you tonight, and I am sure He has. That one talent came in useful, didn't it, Barbara?"

Barbara blushed a little.

"Anyway," she said, "I am glad I shall be able to keep my promise and have something to give Him after all."

ARTHUR MAXWELL

Found in the Swamp

THAT little story about Spot reminds me of another,
about Prince. He was a young black-and-white mon-
grel, and he belonged to Philip, who loved him dearly.

They lived on a farm away out in the country. All
around the house were green fields and woods, while in a
low-lying section a lazy river wandered slowly through a
wide, reed-covered swamp.

One morning when Philip went out to the kennel to take
him his breakfast, Prince was not there.

"That's strange," thought Philip. "I know I put him
in here myself last night. How could he have got away?"

Then he noticed that a loose board had fallen down on
one side, leaving a hole just big enough for Prince to squeeze
through.

"The little scamp!" cried Philip. "Gone hunting on his
own, I suppose. Just wait till I catch him!"

But to his surprise he didn't catch him.

"Prince, Prince!" he called all over the farmyard, but
no Prince answered.

"That's queer," thought Philip. "He's never done anything like this before. Where can he be? Probably he'll
come back during the day."

As Philip had a great deal of work to do for his daddy,
he did not think much about Prince's absence till he returned from the fields in the evening. Then Philip became
anxious.

"What can have happened to him?" he asked daddy.

"I don't know," said daddy. "Maybe he's had a fight
with some other dog and got the worst of it."

51

And that only made Philip more anxious.

"He couldn't have got lost anywhere, could he?"

"Lost!" exclaimed daddy. "Why, no, child. A dog like that would find his way home if you took him twenty miles away."

"Do you think he might have been stolen?"

"I don't see how," said daddy. "Not out here, anyway. Of course, there might be thieves about at night, but I hardly think any one would take Prince, certainly not without a struggle."

When another day had passed with no sign of Prince's return, Philip became really worried. And in his fear he thought of the Lord and prayed very hard that Jesus would somehow help him find Prince again.

Daddy, who wasn't a very good Christian, laughed when he heard about it, and said that he had never heard of lost dogs' being found that way. But Philip and mamma said that though it might seem a strange thing to do, they were going to pray anyway, for surely Jesus must know where the dog was, and could send him back if He thought best.

So they continued to pray for Prince, although as the hours passed it became harder and harder to believe that their prayers could be answered.

On the third night after Prince had disappeared, as Philip was lying in bed in the dark alternately wondering what could have happened to his pet and praying that he might come home again, he heard a strange and terrifying sound that sent a cold shiver down his spine. It wasn't a bark or a yelp, but a fearful wail as of an animal in great distress.

It came again, and this time Philip sat up in bed, a tingling sensation spreading all over his body as though some one were sticking pins and needles into every part of him at once.

When the wail came the third time, he bounded out of bed and ran to his parents' room, knocking loudly on the door.

"What's that?" came a sleepy voice from within.

"Did you hear that noise?" cried Philip, almost beside himself with excitement. "I believe it's Prince."

"What noise?" asked daddy, not too pleased at having been awakened in the middle of the night.

"Listen to it! Oh, I'm sure it's Prince!" cried Philip.

And even as he spoke, the long, low, pitiful wail was borne to them again on the cool night breeze.

There was a thud as daddy jumped out of bed. And another as mamma followed him.

"That came from the swamp as sure as I'm alive," said daddy. "We must go at once and see what's the matter. Quick, light the lanterns."

Philip had his clothes on in less time than it takes to tell and was downstairs lighting the lanterns as daddy and mamma joined him.

Then they set out through the farmyard, down the rough track that led through the grassy meadows toward the river.

"We'll have to take care," said daddy; "this swampy land is very treacherous. More than one animal has been sucked down into these bogs. Follow me carefully and keep to the path."

It was all very eerie, walking through the darkness with only the three lanterns to give them light, the chilly wind sweeping around them, and every now and again the same dreadful wail striking upon their ears.

Now it was getting louder, as they drew nearer. What would they find?

At last daddy called the little procession to a halt.

"I think we're nearly there," he said. "But we must not go any farther. It's too dangerous. Let's wait a moment and listen again."

They waited, standing quite still, and close together.

Suddenly, from almost at their feet, the wail came once more. Mamma and Philip jumped back, they were so scared.

"Shine your lanterns this way," said daddy.

As they did so, they saw the head and shoulders of Prince protruding from the bog into which he was slowly sinking.

"Oh, poor Prince!" cried Philip, darting forward.

"Stand back!" cried daddy, clutching him. "Keep on the path, or you'll go down, too. We'll have to get some planks or a ladder."

"Hurry then!" cried Philip, "or he'll be gone."

They hurried, and a few minutes later poor Prince, covered with slime, and half dead from fright, hunger, and exhaustion, was lying on the firm ground beside them.

As Philip bent over him, patting his wet, muddy head, he flashed a little prayer of gratitude back to heaven. "Thank you, dear Jesus," he whispered, "for hearing my prayer, and sending him back to me."

54

How Lazy Laurie Became Mother's Helper

I WOULDN'T like to say out loud that Laurie was lazy, because probably he would be very much offended; and I don't like to offend anybody. But I am afraid that was the truth.

No matter what it was that you asked Laurie to do, he would invariably reply, "I can't." For every job he seemed to have an excuse. If you asked him to bring in a scuttle of coal, he would say, "I can't; it's too heavy." Or if you asked him to go on an errand, he would say, "I can't; I'm too tired." Perhaps you would ask him to wipe the dishes. Then he would say, "I can't; that's a girl's job."

Of course, there was nothing at all in any of his excuses, and I am quite sure that the real trouble with Laurie was just pure laziness. You see, he said "I can't" only when there was work to be done. He never said it at playtime or when his chum came to the door and asked him to go bicycling or to play ball. Then it was always, "All right, I won't be a tick."

Laurie's mother told him many a time that it wasn't fair that he never helped the least bit in the work of the home and yet was so ready to run off and play. But Laurie was just the same as ever the next day, and all mother had said did not seem to make any difference. But one day mother had a bright idea.

The next morning Laurie stayed in bed so long that he was late for school. Usually mother would call him in good time, only to be answered by a dozy, "I

Laurie was never lazy when "fun" was concerned.

can't get up; I'm sleepy." This morning mother let Laurie get up when he liked; and that was very late indeed. He was cross when he came downstairs, and wanted to have his breakfast immediately. But there was none for him.

"Why didn't you get my breakfast?" he asked.

"I can't," said mother with a curious smile, "I'm so tired."

Very angry, Laurie ran off to school without any breakfast. He was so late that he received two demerit marks, which made him crosser still.

On the way home he climbed a fence with some other boys and, coming down, found himself hooked on to a rusty nail. He managed to get down at last, but left part of his trousers on the top of the fence. When he got home, he wanted mother to mend them at once.

"I can't," said mother. "I'm too busy."

"And have I got to go to school like this?" asked Laurie, pointing to the hole in his trousers.

"I'm afraid so," said mother, and go he had to, greatly to the amusement of the other boys.

When Laurie got back from school, of course he wanted his supper at once, for he had not had much to eat that day. But there was nothing on the table. He was greatly surprised, for he had been used to finding everything ready for him.

"You haven't got the supper ready," he said to mother.

"No," said mother, quite disinterested. "I can't. I'm tired, and the dinner dishes aren't washed yet."

"But I want to go out to play directly after supper," said Laurie.

"All right," said mother, not stirring from her armchair, and looking back at the book she was reading, "I don't mind."

"But aren't you going to get me any supper?"

"I can't; I'm tired."

Laurie stormed out of the house and slammed the door. But as he was going down the street, he began to think things over. Perhaps mother *was* tired after all. Maybe she really did need some one to help her. Perhaps she really was too tired to get her own supper ready.

Laurie stopped. He thought of the game of ball that he was going to enjoy and then of his little mother sitting at home too tired to get her own supper ready. He began to feel sorry that he had been so cross. He would go back.

Peeping through the kitchen window, Laurie saw that mother had gone to sleep in her armchair. At once he realized that this was his opportunity to make things right. At heart he was really a good boy, even though he had that very strong tendency to laziness where work was concerned.

Creeping into the kitchen on tiptoe, he washed up the dishes as silently as he could, and then, still more quietly, crept into the dining room and laid the table. To be quite frank, this was the first time for many months that Laurie had laid the table, but he made a splendid job of it. He put out all the nicest things he could find, brought in some flowers from the garden, and, altogether, made the table look as though some one extra-special was coming in.

Then he noticed that he had forgotten to bring in the butter dish, and went to fetch it. Unfortunately it was a little greasy, and it slipped out of his hands, falling with a crash upon the floor.

Mother awoke and jumped out of her chair as though something dreadful had happened. She had been dreaming about Laurie, and the noise had come just as he had been getting into trouble. But her fears were turned to joy as she realized what Laurie had done.

"Well!" she exclaimed, "who would have believed it!"

They had a lovely meal together, and mother never said a word about the broken butter dish. Laurie was so happy that he determined that he really would help mother more after this.

Just as they were finishing supper, there was a knock at the door, and a boy's voice called out, "Come on, Laurie, we're all waiting for you."

"Sorry I can't come," said Laurie. "I'm going to help mother this evening."

But mother overheard, and she came running to the door.

"It's all right, Laurie, this time. You can help me to-morrow."

Overjoyed, Laurie ran off, and my! that was the best game of ball he ever played.

THE JULIA.

Man Overboard!

MANY a stirring story has been told of the great Lord Nelson, who led the British fleet to many a gallant victory in days of old. You have all read of Trafalgar. Perhaps you have been fortunate enough to see Nelson's flagship in Portsmouth harbor. But here is a story about him that for courage and self-sacrifice outshines perhaps his greatest triumphs.

He was sailing through the Straits of Gibraltar in a small frigate, intent on rejoining the main British fleet stationed some distance out in the Atlantic. Suddenly he was sighted by two Spanish men-of-war. As Spain was at war with Britain, these two ships immediately gave chase to Nelson, hoping to cut him off and destroy his ship before he could reach his fleet.

Nelson, seeing his perilous situation, crowded on all possible sail, hoping against hope that he would come in sight of the fleet before he should be overtaken.

Hour after hour the chase continued, the larger and more powerful Spanish men-of-war slowly but surely overhauling the British ship. Nearer and still nearer they approached. Nelson prepared for action, though he knew the odds were all against him. He would do his best anyway, and certainly, whatever happened, he would never haul down his flag.

Then suddenly the cry was raised, "Man overboard!" Some one had been struck by a heavy sea, and swept over the ship's side.

In those bad old days life was cheap. And in a desperate situation like this, with the enemy drawing nearer every moment and death staring all in the face, who would care that one poor seaman was lost?

The news was carried to Nelson's ears.

"Man overboard, sir," reported an officer.

"Who is it?" asked Nelson.

"Harvey, sir."

"Harvey! We can't afford to lose Harvey!" cried Nelson.

Then, without a moment's hesitation, he gave that heroic command:

"About sail! Lower a boat."

The men stared at him in amazement, but in those days to hear was to obey. Instantly the word was passed through the ship that Harvey was to be rescued at all costs. A boat was lowered, and brave men rowed back, seemingly into the very jaws of death, to rescue the sinking man.

They saved him.

And then a strange thing happened. Suddenly the Spanish ships were seen to alter their course. With a swift movement they turned and fled in the direction whence they had come. They thought, so it was learned afterward, that Nelson must surely have sighted the British fleet, or he never would have turned at such a moment.

So Nelson's self-sacrifice in that desperate moment saved both himself and all his men.

And it often happens so.

ARTHUR MAXWELL

No Marks on God's Glasses

MOTHER had been reading to Jerry out of the Bible. Tonight it had been the story of the woman of Samaria whom Jesus met at the well. They had just reached the place where Jesus says to the woman: "Whosoever drinketh of the water that I shall give him shall never thirst; but the water that I shall give him shall be in him a well of water springing up into everlasting life." John 4:14.

"What does that mean, mamma?" asked Jerry. "How could a well of water spring up? Don't you have to let a bucket down into it?"

"That's a good question," said mamma. "With most wells you do have to let a bucket down, or use a pump, to get the water up; but Jesus says that with His well it is different. The water flows up and over, all on its own, and it keeps on flowing forever."

"But how could it?" asked Jerry.

"Well, darling," said mamma, "this is just a beautiful picture of the love of God for us. His love never stops flowing. It's like a spring that bubbles up out of the ground that no one can stop or like a mighty river that never dries up. We can take all we want of it, bucketfuls and bucketfuls, and after we have taken all we can use there's just as much left as before. No matter how many good things we may receive from Him today as proof of His love, we may know He is ready to bless us even more tomorrow and

H. Hofmann, Artist

Jesus Tells the Woman of Samaria About the Well That Never Runs Dry

the next day and the next day after that, always and always."

"Just like you love me?" asked Jerry.

"Yes, darling, just like that," answered mamma, "only ever so much more. And that reminds me of a story I must tell you."

"Do!" exclaimed Jerry with eagerness, for he loved stories.

"It's about a poor boy who was brought to a hospital the other day. We'll call him Charlie, though that isn't his real name. He was very pale and thin. The doctor said he was half starved, and ordered that he be given plenty to eat to make him well again.

"The nurse brought him a big glass of milk and told him to drink it. But Charlie, looking up anxiously into her face, asked her, 'How deep do I drink?'

" 'How deep!' asked the nurse. 'Whatever do you mean?'

" 'Well, nurse,' said Charlie, 'at home all four of us children have to share the same glass of milk, and mother tells me to drink first because she knows I won't drink too much, and I know where the mark is for me to stop drinking.'

" 'You poor little thing,' said the kindhearted nurse. 'I understand, but you don't have to worry about that here. You may drink all of this. You don't have to watch for any marks.'

"So Charlie drank a whole glassful of milk for the first time in his life. Then he had more and more, for there was no end to the supply of milk the nurses wanted to give him after that.

"And so it is, Jerry," continued mamma, "with the love of God. It is like an everflowing well from which we can keep on drinking without ever fearing that we shall take too much. And when God offers His love to us He doesn't say, 'Drink some of it,' but 'Drink all of it.' And we may be sure that while there is sufficient for all our needs, there is just as much for everybody else in the world.

"There are no marks on God's glasses."

Shirley's Surrender

"I'M just going out for a few minutes, Shirley dear," said mamma. "I won't be long. Be a good girl till I get back."

"Yes, mamma," said Shirley, laying her dolly down in her doll buggy. "Bring some nice cakes back for supper, won't you?"

"I'll see what I can find," said mamma, smiling. "Good-by for ten minutes. Be good, and don't touch anything on the dresser."

"All right, mamma."

Five minutes later, however, Shirley, tired of playing with her dolly, began to look around for something else with which to amuse herself. Wandering slowly around the room, she presently spied a shining object on the dresser. It was mamma's wrist watch, which she had forgotten to take with her.

Shirley picked it up. "I'm sure mamma would not mind my looking at this," she said to herself, " 'cause I have so often looked at it on her wrist."

She turned it over and over, and then decided she would try to fix it on her own wrist. After some struggling, and nearly dropping it three times, she succeeded, and then held up her wrist to admire it.

"Doesn't it look smart?" she said to herself, smiling. "I wish I had a watch like this all my own. I wonder how it winds up?"

Remembering that mamma sometimes turned the little wheel at the side, she decided to do the same,

and began to wind vigorously. Soon it was not only wound up, but overwound, although, of course, Shirley didn't know anything about that.

She had just finished this pleasing little operation when she heard the click of mamma's key in the front door. Like a streak of lightning she undid the strap, put the watch down as nearly as she could remember in the place where she had found it, and hurried back to her dolly.

"Here I am," said mamma. "I haven't been very long, you see. But I couldn't be sure of the time because I left my watch behind. Fancy my forgetting it!"

Mamma walked over to the dresser, picked up her watch, and put it on her wrist. "Funny," she thought to herself, "but I don't remember leaving it face downward. I must have been in a hurry."

Then she looked at it a little more closely.

"Have you brought the cakes for tea?" asked Shirley, with an effort at innocence.

"Yes," said mamma, "some lovely ones. But, Shirley, my watch has stopped. I wonder what can have happened to it?"

Shirley blushed a deep red, and turning her back to mamma, busied herself with her dolly.

"Why!" exclaimed mamma, "It's wound up full. Overwound, I'm afraid. Who could have done it? Has anybody been in while I have been out?"

"No, mamma," said Shirley, still keeping her face out of sight.

"I suppose you didn't touch it," asked mamma.

"No," said Shirley, "I've been playing with my dolly."

"You're quite sure?" persisted mamma, her suspicions now fully aroused.

"Quite sure, mamma. I didn't know your watch was there."

"Shirley," said mamma. "I am very, very sorry, but I don't believe you are telling me the truth."

"I—I—I am," said Shirley, blushing still more deeply.

"Then I think that perhaps it might be better if you went to your bedroom for a little while to think it over," said mamma. "I will come up to see you later."

Shirley, pouting, and protesting her innocence, left the room. The fact was she was glad to go, for she felt very uncomfortable. Having told one falsehood, she felt she had to go on telling others to cover it up. And, as always happens, the more she did that the worse everything became.

It seemed ages before mamma came to her room—long past the usual suppertime. Shirley reflected ruefully that her naughtiness had lost her both cakes and supper, but having gone so far, she felt she couldn't go back. At last the door opened and mamma entered.

"Have you thought it over, Shirley?" she asked quietly. Shirley noticed there were tears in her eyes.

"Yes," said Shirley obstinately, swinging her legs to and fro as she sat on the bed. "I have. And I didn't touch your watch."

"I see," said mamma, sitting down beside the little girl. "But somehow, Shirley, you don't seem very happy about it. If you had not touched my watch,

I think there would have been a different look on your face now."

"But I didn't."

"Shirley, you are only making things worse. If you were just to confess your wrong, you would feel so much happier, and mamma wouldn't be angry."

"But I didn't," repeated Shirley, more softly now, as if she didn't really mean to say it.

"I'm going to tell you a story," said mamma, "and I want you to listen. There was once a little girl who saw a penny at the bottom of a vase, and though she knew it belonged to her mother, she thought she would take it to buy some candy. But when she had put her hand down the narrow neck of the vase, she found she could not get it out again, struggle as she would. At last, very frightened, and thinking she might have to go about with the vase on her hand all her life, she ran to her mother for help—though she did not tell her about the penny. But even her mother could not get her hand out. After making several attempts, she decided to break the vase, costly though it was. When she had broken it, what do you suppose she found?"

"I don't know," said Shirley.

"She found the little girl had the penny grasped tightly in her hand. If only she had dropped the penny, her hand would have come out easily, and the precious vase need not have been broken. But she would not let go. That made all the trouble. And, Shirley, that is what is the matter with you. Pride is keeping you from confessing you have done wrong. Wouldn't you like to 'let go,' and not be obstinate about it any more? After all, it's so much easier to tell the truth, and the only way to be happy again. That is what it says in the Bible, dear: 'He that covereth his sins shall not prosper: but whoso confesseth and forsaketh them shall have mercy.' "

Big tears began to roll down Shirley's cheeks now. "I only put it on my wrist and wound it up," she said, beginning to sob.

"There, there," said mamma soothingly. "I'm glad you've told me at last. Don't you feel happier already?"

Shirley, sniffing hard, nodded her head.

"Yes," she whispered. "I'm sorry I told you all those untruths. And I d—d—don't want to carry an old vase around on my hand all my life."

"That's right," said mamma, smiling. "It's all over now, and I am sure my little Shirley, with Jesus' help, will never say anything untrue in her life again."

"I never will," said Shirley.

"Good girl," said mamma. "Now you must go to bed, and we'll have those cakes for supper to-morrow night."

Why the Difference?

PETER, Paul, and Philip were all about the same size and the same age, and they all lived within a stone's throw of one another.

They had grown up together, playing the same games and going to the same school. Now, being big and husky, they all decided that they ought to do something to help their country; so they went down to the docks and asked for work.

The manager liked the look of the boys and hired them, offering them the same rate of pay.

Several weeks went by. Then one day the three fathers of the boys met and began to compare notes.

"How much is your boy earning?" said Peter's father.

"Twenty dollars a week," said Paul's father. "That isn't so bad for a beginner, and they have given him a five-dollar raise already. What's Peter getting?"

"Only fifteen," said Peter's father in disgust. "I'd like to know why. Doesn't seem fair to me. I wonder what they're paying Philip?"

"I hardly like to say," said Philip's father. "But Philip tells me they have just raised his rate to twenty-five dollars a week."

"Twenty-five!" exclaimed Peter's father, getting quite red in the face. "Just think of that! And Peter is getting only fifteen! I'll go down first thing tomorrow morning and tell the manager what I think of him."

So Peter's father phoned the manager and made an appointment to meet him at ten o'clock the next morning. Every moment till then he became more and more angry as he thought of all the terrible things he would say to the manager when he should meet him.

But the manager guessed why he had come. "I suppose you want to know why your boy is being paid only fifteen dollars a week, while the other two boys from your district have been advanced," he said.

"Yes, indeed," said Peter's father, "and I think it's—"

"Never mind saying what you think," said the manager. "How long can you spend here?"

"Just as long as I have to in order to see that justice is done," said Peter's father.

"Well, it may take an hour or two," said the manager. "Just take a seat in this side room and keep out of sight and watch what happens."

Taken by surprise, Peter's father did not know what else to do but obey. He sat down where he could watch all that went on in the office without himself being observed.

Meanwhile the manager had pressed a button under his desk. Soon the door opened and in walked Peter. His father watched as the boy slouched up to the desk.

"There's a ship just coming in the harbor, due to dock shortly," said the manager. "Get me full particulars and report in half an hour."

"All right," said Peter, and shuffled out.

As minutes slipped by, Peter's father wondered just what sort of report his boy would bring back. Imagine his surprise when, the half hour up, there was no sign of Peter. The boy seemed to have forgotten all about his instructions.

The manager pressed the button again and told a secre-

tary to send for Paul. The boy arrived and stood atten-
tively in front of the manager's desk.

"There's a ship just coming in the harbor, due to dock
shortly," repeated the manager. "Get me full particulars
and report in half an hour."

Again the minutes slipped by. As the time limit was
almost up, Paul returned.

"The ship has just docked, sir," he said. "She's a big
ship and quite heavily loaded with cargo."

"Is that all?"

"That's all."

"Thank you. You may go."

Then the manager pressed his bell the third time and
after a brief pause in came Philip.

"Good morning, sir," said the boy with a smile. "What
may I do for you, sir?"

The manager repeated his request for full particulars
about the incoming ship and asked Philip to be back as soon
as possible with the information.

Twenty minutes later Philip was back in the manager's
office again.

"Well, Philip," said the manager, "what did you find
out about that ship?"

"She's a 10,000-ton freighter, sir. Last port of call
was Cape Town, South Africa. She docked at 10:10
A. M. Cargo chiefly oranges and other fruit. There are a
hundred men busy unloading her now, sir. The captain
wants to sail again one week from tonight. Repairs are
needed to the radio and in the boiler room."

"Thank you, Philip, that is what I wanted to know.
You are excused."

"And now," said the manager, turning to Peter's father,

"do you require any further explanation of the difference in wage rates?"

"No, I don't," said Peter's father. "But I would like to know where Peter is and why he did not come back."

"So would I," said the manager. "Perhaps you can find out why he loafs on his job."

"I think you can leave that to me," said Peter's father, with a purposeful tone in his voice. "I'll look after him."

And he did.

The Little Bird That Tells

"How is it that mamma knows so much?" said Connie to Vera as they sat in their little "cubby-house" in the garden. "Every time we do anything naughty, she seems to know all about it beforehand."

"I don't know," said Vera. "She always says that 'a little bird' tells her. I'd like to catch the bird."

"So would I," said Connie. "I suppose it can't be the parrot."

"Our parrot doesn't talk," said Vera.

"Perhaps the canary, then," smiled Connie.

"Whoever heard of a canary's talking?" said Vera.

"Well, I'd like to catch it anyway," said Connie.

"And so would I," said Vera.

Just then mamma called from the house, and both little girls ran to answer.

"Come, dears," said mamma, "I want you both to go shopping for me. Here's a list of things and here's a dollar, which should be quite enough. Now hurry along and come straight back, as I want some of the things for dinner."

The two girls were delighted to go, especially at being trusted to spend the money themselves. Cheerily they waved their hands to mamma, and hurried out of the gate.

Soon they reached the market, and it was not long before all the things on the list were purchased.

" Haven't we finished quickly! " said Connie.

" Mamma won't expect us back so soon," said Vera. " Perhaps we could stay a minute or two and look in the windows."

" Well, just a minute," said Connie. " Mamma wouldn't mind that."

So they stopped a minute and looked; and the minute lengthened into five minutes, then ten minutes, then fifteen minutes.

" Look at that sweet little chocolate chicken," said Vera. " Shall we get it? "

" But you haven't any money."

" No, but the potatoes didn't cost as much as mamma put down on the list, and I'm sure she wouldn't mind."

" I'm not so sure," said Connie, " but it is pretty. You get it."

In a moment Vera was in the shop and out again, with the chocolate chicken in a paper bag. They divided it between them, and ate it as they started off leisurely toward home.

" Say, look at that clock, Vera," exclaimed Connie. " We'd better run. I didn't know we had been so long."

So away they sped, rushing up the path and into the house with the basketful of goods.

" Here they are, mamma dear," said Connie, " I hope we haven't been too long."

" I did think you would be back a little before this," said mamma.

" Well, you know, mamma," said Vera, blushing just a little, " it always takes the vegetable man a long time to weigh out his potatoes."

" Sometimes," said mamma with an understanding look. " And this is the change? "

" Yes, mamma."

Somehow they couldn't bring themselves to mention the chocolate chicken, even though they had been so sure that " mamma wouldn't mind." Both began to feel distinctly uncomfortable.

An hour later dinner was served. For some reason or other it did not please the girls a bit.

" I don't like this sort of dinner," said Vera. " And we always seem to have the same — potatoes and greens, and greens and potatoes —."

" Can't you get us a really nice dinner some day soon? " asked Connie. " I'm tired of this sort of thing too. Really, I can't eat it to-day."

Mamma said very little, but she was beginning to put two and two together. After dinner she called both girls into the living room.

" Children," she said, " what did you have to eat in town this morning? "

" To eat, mamma? " said Vera with affected surprise.

" Now, darlings, don't make it worse by telling falsehoods. You have been tempted to do something that was wrong, and I believe mamma knows all about it."

Both girls began to blush deeply.

" You stayed looking at the shops in town," said mamma kindly, but seriously, " and you also bought some sweets with some of the change you should have brought back to me. Is that right? "

Tears were trickling down their cheeks now.

"O mamma!" cried Connie, "how did you know?"

"Oh," said mamma, "a little bird —"

"Don't say that, mamma," said Vera. "Tell us how you know, for you always know everything."

"Well, then, dears, *you* told me. I saw it in your eyes and in your cheeks. I heard it in your voices at dinner time. You were the little bird. Conscience was making cowards of you. You were afraid to look your own mamma straight in the face. I knew all about it the moment you came into the house."

"O mamma!" cried Connie, "we'll never, never try to deceive you any more. It was so mean of us."

"You are gladly forgiven, dears, but remember that we cannot cover up wrong-doing. 'Be sure your sin will find you out.' The little bird will surely betray you. As Solomon says, however secret we may think we have made our sin, 'a bird of the air shall carry the voice, and that which hath wings shall tell the matter.'" Eccl. 10: 20.

The Stoneboat

THIS is a story about a strange sort of boat that never floats on water. Instead, it goes on land!

It is called a "stoneboat," and yet it is not made of stone, but of wood.

If you happen to live on a farm where there is a great deal of stony land, then you will know exactly what I mean; but in case you don't, perhaps I had better tell you.

A stoneboat is made of several heavy planks of wood stoutly nailed together and slightly curved at one end. It is really a sort of flat platform drawn by a horse, and used to carry away stones from the fields.

You see, where land is shallow and rocky, there is likely to be a number of big stones lying on or near the surface every spring, and the farmer likes to clear them away before he gets his plows to work. Sometimes the stoneboat is used in the opening up of new land, and then quite heavy boulders will be lifted on to it and hauled away.

Well, Leslie and Donovan were sent out with a stoneboat one day by their father, with orders to clear a certain field of stones.

The two boys rather enjoyed the job, and were soon working with a will. They liked to see the field gradually looking cleaner as they piled up the stones on the stoneboat and dumped them in a near-by dell. They felt that they were really helping father, and they knew how pleased he would be when the job was done.

All day long they worked out in the field, and by late afternoon they were feeling rather tired. It was almost time to quit and return home. Unexpectedly they came across a big and obstinate rock. It didn't look so big at first, for there was only a very little of it showing above the ground. But when they tried to move it, they found it was very large and was deeply buried.

Leslie took the crowbar they always carried with them for jobs like this and tried to lever it out. But it wouldn't move. They both got hold of the crowbar and heaved on it, but still the rock refused to budge.

"Oh, I'm too tired to move this one today," said Leslie. "Let's leave it. I won't have strength enough to play ball with the fellows this evening. Come on, let's go."

"All right," said Donovan. "We've picked up enough rocks anyway today. But what will father say if he sees this one left here?"

"Cover it over with earth, and then he won't see," said Leslie. "Then we'll come back tomorrow and take it away."

So they covered up the rock, and drove away with the last load on the stoneboat.

And, of course, they both forgot all about that rock. In fact, they did not think of it again until some days later, when father met them with a frown on his brow.

"Just broke my plow," he said. "Hit a rock up there in that field you two were supposed to have cleared."

Leslie and Donovan blushed as it all came back to their minds.

"Funny thing," said father, "that rock was only just under the surface. In fact, when I looked it over afterward it seemed to me that it had only recently been covered up."

The two boys looked away. There was nothing they could say.

By this time father had his suspicions; so he went on: "There is a text in the Bible which says, 'Be sure your sin will find you out.' And it seems to me that somebody's sin has been found out today."

Still the two boys remained silent.

"Well, boys," father continued, "I don't know what you did or didn't do, and it's too late now to alter things. But I want you to remember that those rocks are just like sins. Some can be picked up and got rid of without much trouble, but others are lodged deep down, with only a small part of them showing above the surface. You can't get rid of those by just covering them up. You have to dig them out, and the sooner the better. If you don't, there is always the chance that somebody will run into them and show them up; and if that doesn't happen, you can be dead sure that next year, after the winter rains, they will appear again as bare and ugly as ever. Deep-rooted sins must be dug out right away, as soon as they are found. And if you cannot move them with your own crowbar, you had better ask father to come and help."

"Thanks, dad," said the boys. "We understand, and we won't leave any rocks in the field next time."

The Angel of the Books

"WHAT dreadful language you are bringing into this house, Tom," said mother one day. "Why, even Joan and Jess are calling each other 'little beasts' and things like that. It's got to stop."

"Can't help it," said Tom, who had just started going to school. "All the boys call each other names."

"But you mustn't do it, Tom. You must be different, and set the other boys a good example."

"Can't," said Tom. "They're all bigger than I am, and they won't listen to me."

"That may be," said mamma, "but you don't need to use the same language as the other boys. Anyhow, you mustn't use it in this house, that's sure."

"Oh, blow!" said Tom.

"Tom!" exclaimed mother. "That's the last time you have said that here."

"Oh, blow!" came an echo from the dining room.

"There!" said mother. "There's little Joan learning that from you now. I won't have it. The next time you use any of those idle words, you shall go straight to bed without any supper."

"Beastly mean!" muttered Tom under his breath.

"That's enough," said mother. "Up you go."

"But I was just going out to play football."

"Doesn't matter. It is much more important

to learn that you must not use bad language."

Tom sauntered slowly upstairs and into his bedroom. More slowly still he undressed and got into bed. He didn't mind going to bed so much, but the fact that there was to be no supper was too much for him. Tears began to trickle down his cheeks. He tossed and turned, wiped his eyes, put the handkerchief under his pillow, and pulled it out again. Gradually he dozed off.

Hello! Who was this in his bedroom? He rubbed his eyes and sat up, very much frightened.

" Who are you? " he asked.

" I am the Angel of the Books," said the visitor.

" Books! " gasped Tom. " What books? "

" The books of heaven," said the angel. " I record every idle word that men speak."

" Good Lor'," said Tom.

" That also will be written down."

" Mustn't I say that? "

" It is very wrong. Have you not read, ' Thou shalt not take the name of the Lord thy God in vain '? "

" I'm sorry," said Tom. " I won't say it any more."

" You will not be able to," said the angel. " You have said so many bad words of late that you must be silent for a long time. Good-by."

The angel disappeared. Tom, very much frightened, tried to call mother and tell her about what he had seen, but he could not speak. It was terrible. He wanted to tell mother how sorry he was for being rude to her, but he couldn't say a word. He remembered how mean he had been to his auntie, and wanted to go and ask her pardon, but not a word could he utter. Then he thought of dear little Jess and Joan. How he wanted to go and tell them a story, and be nice to them to make up for teasing them so much, but he could not. Not a word would come from his lips.

" Oh, dear! " he thought. " Shall I never be able to speak again? "

He saw mother lying in bed very ill, and heard the doctor come and say how sick she was. He heard people come upstairs bringing fruit and flowers to cheer her up. He heard all the kind things they said to her. How he longed to go to her bedside and tell her he would try to be a good boy, and how he, too, wanted her to be well again, but his tongue would not move.

Ah! Here was the angel back again.

" I believe you have learned your lesson," said the Angel of the Books.

Tom nodded his head, while tears ran down his face.

" If you promise to try hard never to use a bad word again," said the angel, " you may speak."

Tom nodded his head, the gift of speech returned, and the angel disappeared once more.

*   *   *   *   *

" What's the matter, dearie? " said mother, bending over him.

" O mother dear! " cried Tom, " I've had such a wonderful and terrible dream. And I do love you so much, and I'll never, never use bad words again."

Jane's Plot

A Christmas Story

THERE was an air of mystery about the manse. To be quite accurate, it was chiefly in the garage.

This garage was once a stable, large, light, and warm. At one end was the minister's car, at the other a playroom for Jane, Bob, and Kiki. Kiki was the dog. I hope you can find him in the picture.

It was late in December, and everybody, as usual, was talking about Christmas presents. Jane and Bob wanted so many things that they found it difficult to decide what they wanted most. So they went out to their committee room to talk it over. Father was always attending committees, so they thought it would be proper to do the same.

"Now what is it going to be?" asked Jane when all three were comfortably seated in the garage.

"I don't know," said Bob. "Now father's got this car he says he hasn't any money left for Christmas presents."

"Well, I've got several dollies," said Jane, "but I simply *must* have a new one, because my favorite has lost its hair and its eyes have fallen in."

"That's soon settled then," said Bob. "But what about me? I don't know what to ask for. I've got engines and rails and boats and things, and, well, I don't know."

"Snowshoes," suggested Jane. "Those you saw in the shop last week that father said were too expensive."

"That will do; now write your letter. We mustn't ask for any more or we won't get anything."

Together they made a desk out of an old barrel and a piece of wood, and Jane sat herself down to write to "Father Christmas." She had got down as far as "snowshoes" when the piece of wood tipped up, and the ink bottle shot off on to the floor with a big splash.

"Oh, you naughty, naughty Kiki," said Jane.

"He's all right, he only kick-eed it," laughed Bob. "Perhaps he wanted a present too."

"Oh, yes; we had quite forgotten him," said Jane. "Let us ask for a new collar for him. But he doesn't deserve it after spilling the ink all over the floor. And look! All my letter is covered with blots! You bad dog!"

However, Jane added a request for Kiki, and then signed her letter. But the blots were so big they would not dry, so she left them in disgust.

"Let's ask mamma if we can go down town to see the shops," she said.

"Let's," said Bob, and away they went, Kiki at their heels.

Mamma said "Yes," and they were soon on their way to town, feasting their eyes on all the pretty things to be seen in the shop windows.

There was one place where all children delighted to go, for they were always allowed to go inside and walk all the way around without anybody's saying they mustn't. It was called the children's paradise.

Slowly they moved around until they came to a section where there were a toy motor car and some big animals on wheels, and a princess driving a horse and trap.

"See," said Bob, "that car's the same color as father's."

"Yes," said Jane, "and that horse in the trap is just like the one I had last year. And see, there's a gun like yours."

"Yes," said Bob, "and do you remember when I had one of those elephants on wheels?"

"Wasn't it a funny thing!" replied Jane, "and it has lost one of its legs now."

As they talked happily together, they gradually became aware of the presence of another boy and girl who were also looking at the same things.

"My word, Elsie," said the boy, "wouldn't I like that motor car!"

"O Jack!" said the little girl, "just look at those beautiful dollies! And the princess in the cart. Doesn't she look wonderful!"

"No luck," said Jack, "they're not for us. They're only for the rich people's children."

"I know," sighed Elsie, "but I do wish I could have just one of those lovely dollies."

"Yes, but they're five and six," said the boy, "and we daren't spend that on a doll, even if we had that much."

Tears began to trickle down the little girl's face.

"I know," she said, trying to be brave.

"Never mind, Elsie," said the boy, tenderly; "one day when I get big I will go to work and earn money enough to buy you the best doll in the world. Trust me for that."

Just then Jane, who had overheard the last few sentences, looked round and stared full into the pretty, tear-stained face of little Elsie. It was but a momentary glance, and both looked away quickly, but Jane's heart had been touched.

"O Bob," she whispered, "I want to cry."

"Well, don't do it here," said Bob.

"But, Bob, didn't you hear what they were saying? I didn't know people could be so poor. And look, see their awful clothes."

"Let's pass on," said Bob.

He took Jane's arm and drew her toward the next show room.

"Bob," said Jane, her mind working quickly, "I can't forget that poor little girl's face. Can't we do something ——?"

"But they've gone now," said Bob, not unkindly, but a little impatiently.

"Come, Bob, let us follow them," said Jane, now master of the situation, and with a big purpose growing in her heart, "let us follow them and find out where they live."

Bob was always game for an adventure, and he knew that when Jane planned something, he might just as well follow first as last.

Quickly they retraced their steps, catching up with Jack and Elsie as they were going out of the door. Keeping a few paces behind them, they followed on, up one street and down another, until they found themselves at last in a very poor section of the town. They saw Jack and Elsie enter a dingy little dwelling such as Bob and Jane would not have thought fit for an outhouse.

"Oh dear!" exclaimed Jane. "Fancy having to live in such a place! What is the number? Twenty-six."

"Umph!" said Bob. "Not likely to get many Christmas presents there."

"No, and she had such a dear face," said Jane.

Half an hour later Jane and Bob were back in the garage. All the way home Jane had been developing her "plot." All thought of their own desires was completely forgotten, now that this new and beautiful idea had come to them. The big problem was how to earn enough money between now and Christmas eve to make it successful. Father was besieged with requests for permission to clean the car — at a price. Mother had help of all kinds thrust upon her. Little by little the fund grew.

*　　*　　*　　*　　*

"Cold night," said Jack as he and Elsie and their little brother and sister crowded close to the kitchen grate in 26 Mill Street. It was Christmas eve.

"Some people must be having a good time," said little Elsie.

"You're thinking about those things we saw in the shops," said Jack.

"Yes," said Elsie. "Weren't they grand? Do you remember those two children who were there when we looked at the dolls and the motor car? What a kind face the little girl had! I wish I could see her again some day."

"You'll never do that," said Jack. "She's out at a party to-night, all dressed up like a fairy or something, eating fine cakes and pies."

Silence followed, while little Elsie's cheeks began to get wet again.

"What's that?" exclaimed Jack. "Motors don't often come up here at this time of night."

"And there's a dog barking at the door," said Elsie. "What can it be?"

Rat-a-tat-tat!

Jack sprang up to open the door, and in burst two jolly children, clad in warm overcoats and laden with parcels. Their faces were red with the cold and beaming with joy, while around their legs jumped a quaint little dog, who seemed as excited as the children and determined to trip everybody up.

"Why, it's the little girl who smiled at me in the shop," cried Elsie. "How did you find us here?"

"Look," cried Jane, " here are some of the things you wanted. We've saved up for them ever since we saw you. And mother has sent this for dinner to-morrow. A happy Christmas to all of you — and — good-by."

Elsie was in tears now, she was so happy. It was too much for Jane. She gave Elsie a kiss, and waving her hand to all the others, ran out to the car.

"Thank you —" began Jack, following them out.

"Good-by," shouted Jane and Bob.

"Yap-yap," barked Kiki.

"Honk, honk," said father with his horn.

And they were off.

In the morning, though in the joy and excitement of their great idea they had forgotten to post the ink-bespattered letter in the garage, Jane found beside her bed a more beautiful dollie than she had ever dared to hope for, Bob found his snowshoes and something else besides, and even Kiki had a collar.

Now tell me, pray, how " Father Christmas " knew just what to send, after all?